ANOTHER TITLE FROM
FRANCES LINCOLN CHILDREN'S BOOKS

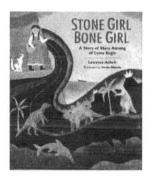

Stone Girl, Bone Girl
A Story of Mary Anning of Lyme Regis
Laurence Anholt
Illustrated by Sheila Moxley

Mary Anning is probably the world's best-known fossil-hunter. As a little girl, she found a fossilised sea monster, an Ichthyosaurus, the most important prehistoric discovery of its time.

Frances Lincoln titles are available from all good bookshops.
You can also buy books and find out more about your favourite titles,
authors and illustrators on our website: www.franceslincoln.com

Mary Anning did become famous.

After finding the Ichthyosaur, she went on to make many more important finds, including two complete Plesiosaurs and the first Pterodactyl ever found in Britain. Even though she never went to school and never left Lyme Regis, she made an international reputation as a fossil expert. She died in 1847 at the age of 48.

Mary lived at a time when scientists were working on a new idea — that the world was much older than they had always thought. This shocked some people, as it seemed to contradict what was written in the Bible. Mary's discoveries helped provide the evidence that the scientists needed to back up their new ideas.

In 1859, twelve years after Mary died, Charles Darwin's book The Origin of Species by Means of Natural Selection was published. His theory of evolution sparked off a revolution in religious and scientific thought, and its effects are still felt to this day.

Without Mary Anning and her fossils, the history of science might have been very different.

Just when Mary and Joe thought the last sightseer had gone, a figure appeared at the door. It was Henry Henley, Lord of the Manor.

He was very interested to see the curiosity, and told them that the creature was not a crocodile . . .

... while outside, a very long queue was forming.

Mary and Joe charged each person a penny to see the curiosity.
Now they could afford their first hot meal for months.

Then as the cart pulled away across the beach, there was a sudden CRACK — and the tower collapsed like a pack of cards!

Mary lowered all the pieces down into Mr Arkwright's cart, and took one last look at the hole where the curiosity had been buried all those years.

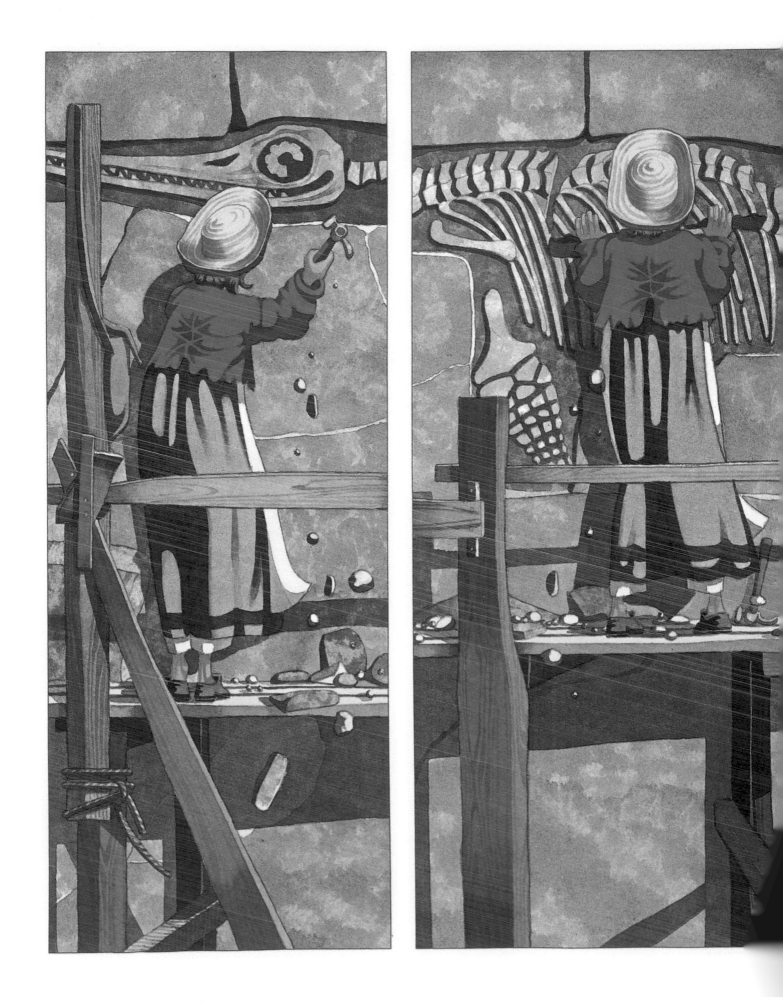

Or stupid.

Rrrfff!

When the tower was ready, Mary climbed up the rickety ladder. The platform swayed under her. It was a long, long way down.

Oo-er.

Then she turned to face the creature.

That night, Mary lay awake thinking of a way to get her crocodile down the cliff and into the shop. Next morning . . .

I've got an idea! I wonder if Mr Arkwright would build me a tower?

You're mad.

Mary picked some flowers for Mr Arkwright, and asked him if he would build her a tower up the cliff. He was so intrigued, he said yes.

Thank you, thank you, thank you, Mr Arkwright!

Mr Arkwright from up the hill came to repair the damage. Then Mary and Joe set out to find some new curiosities.

All the curiosities were swept away.

Don't worry, Mama. Joe and I will soon find more curiosities. We'll start tomorrow.

And then suddenly, in the middle of the night, a huge wave burst through the windows, flooding the Annings' house.

The FOSSIL GIRL

Mary Anning's Dinosaur Discovery

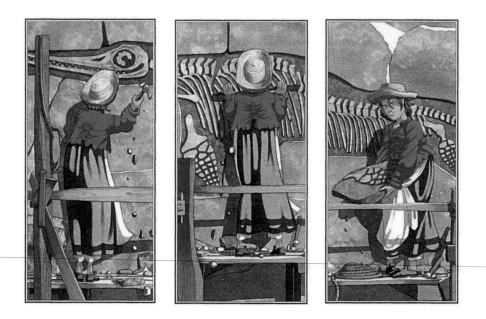

Catherine Brighton

FRANCES LINCOLN
CHILDREN'S BOOKS

Quarto is the authority on a wide range of topics.

Quarto educates, entertains and enriches the lives of
our readers—enthusiasts and lovers of hands-on living.

www.quartoknows.com

For George Short

The right of Catherine Brighton to be identified as the author and illustrator
of this Work has been asserted by her in accordance with the
Copyright, Designs and Patents Act, 1988 (United Kingdom).
First published in Great Britain and the USA in 1999 by
Frances Lincoln Children's Books, 74-77 White Lion Street,
London N1 9PF
www.franceslincoln.com

First published in paperback in 2007

A catalogue record for this book is available from the British Library

ISBN 13: 978-1-84507-732-7

Illustrated with watercolour

Set in Gill Sans and Perpetua

Printed in the UK

CATHERINE BRIGHTON studied at St Martin's School of Art
and the Royal College of Art in London. Her first book for Frances Lincoln,
was described by *The Junior Bookshelf* as a "volume of real enchantment".
Catherine lives in London with her family.